Mr Brown's Magnificent Apple Tree

Yvonne Winer

Illustrated by Maya Winters

AN ASHTON ORIGINAL

from Ashton Scholastic
Sydney Auckland New York Toronto London

National Library of Australia
Cataloguing-in-Publication data

Winer, Yvonne.
    Mr Brown's magnificent apple tree.

    For children.
    ISBN 0 86896 303 8

    I. Winters, Maya, illus. II. Title

    A.823'.3

First published in 1985 by Ashton Scholastic Pty Limited (Inc. in NSW),
PO Box 579, Gosford 2250. Also in Brisbane, Melbourne, Adelaide, Perth
and Auckland, NZ.

Typeset by G.T. Setters Pty Ltd

Printed in Hong Kong

6543   789/8

Mr Brown had a magnificent apple tree.
On this tree hung five ripe, red apples.
Each day,
Mr Brown went out to count the apples.

1, 2, 3, 4, 5!
Five ripe, red apples.

One night, a tiny, grey mouse
ran up the trunk of the tree.
Tip, tap!
Tip, tap!
She chewed through the stem
of one apple.

"PLOP!"

It fell to the ground
where the mouse family was waiting.

Nibble,
nibble,
nibble.
The mouse family soon ate up
every piece of the apple
then scampered back home.

The next morning,
Mr Brown came out of his house
and counted the apples.

1, 2, 3, 4! Only 4 apples!

'A tall, tall thief
must have come in the night
and stolen my apple,' he said.
He went back into his house,
very puzzled.

Late that night,
when everything was quiet,
the tiny, grey mouse
ran further up the trunk of the tree.

Tip, tap!
Tip, tap!
Tip, tap!
She chewed through the stem
of another apple.

PLOP!

It fell to the ground.

Nibble,
nibble,
nibble.
The mouse family
soon ate up every piece of that apple
then scampered back home.

The next morning,
Mr Brown came out of his house
and counted the apples.

1, 2, 3! Only 3 apples left!

'An even taller thief
must have come in the night
and stolen my apple,' he said.
He went back into his house, very puzzled.

That night,
when everything was quiet,
the tiny mouse
ran up the trunk of the tree —
even further up than the night before.

Tip, tap!
Tip, tap!
Tip, tap!
Tip, tap!

She chewed through the stem
of another apple.

"*PLOP!*"

It fell to the ground where the mouse family was waiting.

The mouse family
soon ate up every piece
of that juicy apple
then scampered back home.

The next morning,
Mr Brown came out of his house
and counted the apples.

1, 2! Only 2 apples left!

'I can't believe it!
I think a GIANT
must have come in the night
and stolen my apple!'

Mr Brown
wanted to see the giant thief
who had stolen his apples.
That night, after it was dark,
he crept out of his house.
He hid behind a bush and waited.

When everything was quiet,
the tiny mouse
ran up the trunk of the tree.

Tip, tap! Tip, tap!
Tip, tap! Tip, tap!
She chewed through the stem.

Mr Brown watched in amazement.

"PLOP!"

It fell down
to where the mouse family was waiting.
Nibble, nibble, nibble.
The mouse family
soon ate up every piece of that apple
then scampered back home.
Mr Brown went back into his house,
shaking his head.

Next morning, he got out the ladder,
climbed up and picked the last apple.
He ate every piece of it.

That night, the little mice
peered out of their holes and squealed,
'A GIANT has stolen our last apple!'